D1297090

Petri's Next Things

Written by Christy Cashman

Illustrated by Regina Walsh

JPIC
7/21

Proudly printed in the United States of America.

First Printing, 2020

Blue Sky Publishing
54 W 40th St
New York, NY 10018

www.BlueSkyPublisher.com

Petri's Next Things

Written by Christy Cashman

Illustrated by Regina Walsh

Petri was a very busy monkey.

He was so busy, he made himself a list
—a list of all the things he had to do.

He carried the list with him wherever he
went, even when he brushed his teeth . . .

. . . and ate his breakfast.

Petri loved putting a big, giant check mark next to the things he did so he could move on to the next thing on his list.

He was very proud of his list.

When Petri went to bed, he checked
"Go to sleep." Sometimes he checked
"Have sweet dreams."

One day, at Percival the Pigeon's birthday party, the other animals wondered why he wanted to leave early. "Why are you rushing off?" asked Finn the Fish. "Where do you have to go?" asked Marvin the Mouse.

"The next thing," replied Petri.
"I have to do the next thing."

"Ahhhhh, the next thing. The next thing
is very important," they all agreed.

All of the animals looked where Petri was
pointing, but they couldn't see his next things.

"My next things are out there," said Petri,
"and they all have to be checked off my list."

Petri rolled up his list of next things and
prepared to leave the birthday party.

"But . . . what if you don't do the next things?" asked Percy the Pigeon. "What would happen then?"

"It would be very bad," said Petri. And
he rushed off to do his next thing.

His friends wanted to know where he was
rushing off to, but he was too busy to answer.

The next thing, The next thing has to get done

The only thing on Petri's mind was his next thing.

Petri's friends only had one or two things
to do every day. They didn't even
need to make a list.

On his way to his next thing, Petri stopped under the oak tree by the river to put a big check mark next to "Percy the Pigeon's birthday party." "Done," he said. "On to the next thing."

He sat in the tree and looked for the
next thing on his list.

Just then, a gust of wind blew his list of
next things into the river. "Oh, no!"
cried Petri. "My next things!"

Petri's friends heard him. They all tried to
help. They followed the list of next things
as it floated down the river. Doris the Donkey
gave Petri a stick. Marvin the Mouse tried
to fish it out with his fishing rod. But
the list of next things floated away.

Everyone was very sad for Petri.
They all knew how important his list
of next things was to him.

Just then, Doris the Donkey arrived with
fresh new paper. "Here you go, Petri.
You can start a new list." Petri looked at
the blank paper and thanked Doris.

Suddenly, Percy the Pigeon flew in.
"I was flying over the river just beyond the
bridge, and I found your list of next things
caught on a branch of the willow tree!"

Everyone celebrated. Everyone
except Petri.

His friends wanted to know what was wrong. "We thought you would be thrilled that we found your important list of next things," they all said.

Petri thought about the last few hours.
His friends had all tried so hard to help him.
He thought about how sad they'd felt for him
and how they'd all stopped whatever they'd
been doing because they knew how much he
cared about his list of next things.

He felt bad for always leaving them to rush off to the next thing. "I've decided that next things can wait," he said. "I want to be here. I want to be here right now."

"It doesn't matter," he said.
"Right now is all that matters."

The End.

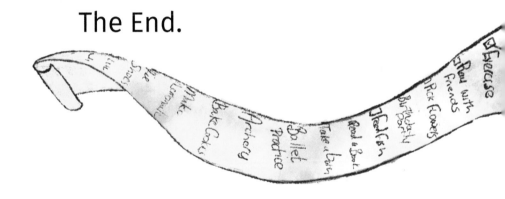

About The Author, Christy Cashman

Christy grew up in North Carolina as part of a large family, the second youngest of ten children.

As a little girl, Christy dreamed of owning the dairy farm across the road and turning it into her very own horse farm. Little did she realize that when she grew up she would get to vacation often in an Irish castle (with a legend about a very smart monkey)!

So far, Christy has authored two children's books – *The Not-So-Average Monkey of Kilkea Castle* and *Petri's Next Things*. She's also written a novel called *The Truth About Horses* (scheduled for release in 2021), and in 2018 wrote an article series, *Horses I Have Known*, about some of her amazing adventures on horseback. Christy is also an American actress, producer, director, and screenwriter, and has appeared in over twenty Hollywood feature films.

Christy lives with her husband, Jay; two sons, Jay Michael and Quinn; three dogs, Ben, Lucy, and Dan; and three horses, Calvin, Butterscotch, and Lance. The family spends their time between Kilkea Castle and their homes in Boston and Chatham, Massachusetts.

You can read more about Christy on her website **www.ChristyCashman.com**

About The Illustrator, Regina Walsh

Regina is a graphic artist and illustrator originally from Tullamore Co. in Offaly, Ireland. She now lives in Kilkenny. Regina works with both traditional and print media, and she loves creating vibrant illustrations that capture your imagination.

About Kilkea Castle – Petri's Home

On a lush, rolling hilltop among the greenest meadows in all of Ireland, not far from Dublin, you'll find fairies playing leapfrog and leprechauns muttering to themselves as they scout for treasure. And you'll also find a very magical castle called Kilkea Castle.

Built over 840 years ago, Kilkea Castle's thick flagstone walls and soaring turrets are everything you dream of when you imagine a castle: secret passages, spiral staircases, coats of armor, and an ancient history that whispers of many secrets. Have you heard the tales of the castle's wizard earl who transformed into a raven? Or the warrior earl called Hump-Backed John who vigorously defended its walls? Or perhaps you've heard of the most famous legend of all – the story of the brave castle monkey who saved the day . . .

Long ago, the owners of the castle, the Fitzgerald Family, had a 'cheeky' pet monkey who used to escape and hide in the trees around the castle grounds. No matter what they did to keep the monkey from running away, he always managed to disappear. To keep the naughty monkey contained, the Fitzgeralds put him on a chain and kept him in the nursery, which was located on the top floor of the castle.

One night, as the Fitzgeralds held a family gathering, a fire broke out. Baby John, the 1st Earl of Kildare, was fast asleep in the nursery – along with the monkey. The family was frantic as the flames erupted and they could not reach John. Suddenly, the monkey appeared, carrying baby John in his arms. He had saved him! The Earl, in appreciation, adopted the monkey's image for the family's crest, which you can see today in the Kilkea Castle logo. And if you visit Kilkea Castle, look to the right of the chimney. You will see a carving of the brave little monkey who saved the day. The Castle has seen no fire since.

Learn more about Kilkea Castle, and come visit us! **www.kilkeacastle.ie**